Animals with Armor

Beetles

by Julie Murray

Dash!
LEVELED READERS
An Imprint of Abdo Zoom • abdobooks.com

Dash!
LEVELED READERS

Level 1 – Beginning
Short and simple sentences with familiar words or patterns for children who are beginning to understand how letters and sounds go together.

Level 2 – Emerging
Longer words and sentences with more complex language patterns for readers who are practicing common words and letter sounds.

Level 3 – Transitional
More developed language and vocabulary for readers who are becoming more independent.

THIS BOOK CONTAINS RECYCLED MATERIALS

abdobooks.com

Published by Abdo Zoom, a division of ABDO, PO Box 398166, Minneapolis, Minnesota 55439. Copyright © 2022 by Abdo Consulting Group, Inc. International copyrights reserved in all countries. No part of this book may be reproduced in any form without written permission from the publisher. Dash!™ is a trademark and logo of Abdo Zoom.

Printed in the United States of America, North Mankato, Minnesota.
102021
012022

Photo Credits: iStock, Shutterstock
Production Contributors: Kenny Abdo, Jennie Forsberg, Grace Hansen, John Hansen
Design Contributors: Candice Keimig, Neil Klinepier

Library of Congress Control Number: 2021940129

Publisher's Cataloging in Publication Data
Names: Murray, Julie, author.
Title: Beetles / by Julie Murray.
Description: Minneapolis, Minnesota : Abdo Zoom, 2022 | Series: Animals with armor | Includes online resources and index.
Identifiers: ISBN 9781098226589 (lib. bdg.) | ISBN 9781644946541 (pbk.) | ISBN 9781098227425 (ebook) | ISBN 9781098227845 (Read-to-Me ebook)
Subjects: LCSH: Beetles--Juvenile literature. | Insects--Juvenile literature. | Armored animals--Juvenile literature. | Animal defenses--Juvenile literature. | Veterinary anatomy--Juvenile literature.
Classification: DDC 595.76--dc23

Table of Contents

Beetles 4

More Facts 22

Glossary 23

Index 24

Online Resources 24

Beetles

Beetles are insects. They are found all over the world.

Beetles can live on land or in fresh water.

7

They come in all sizes. The Hercules beetle is the longest. It is about seven inches (17.8 cm) long!

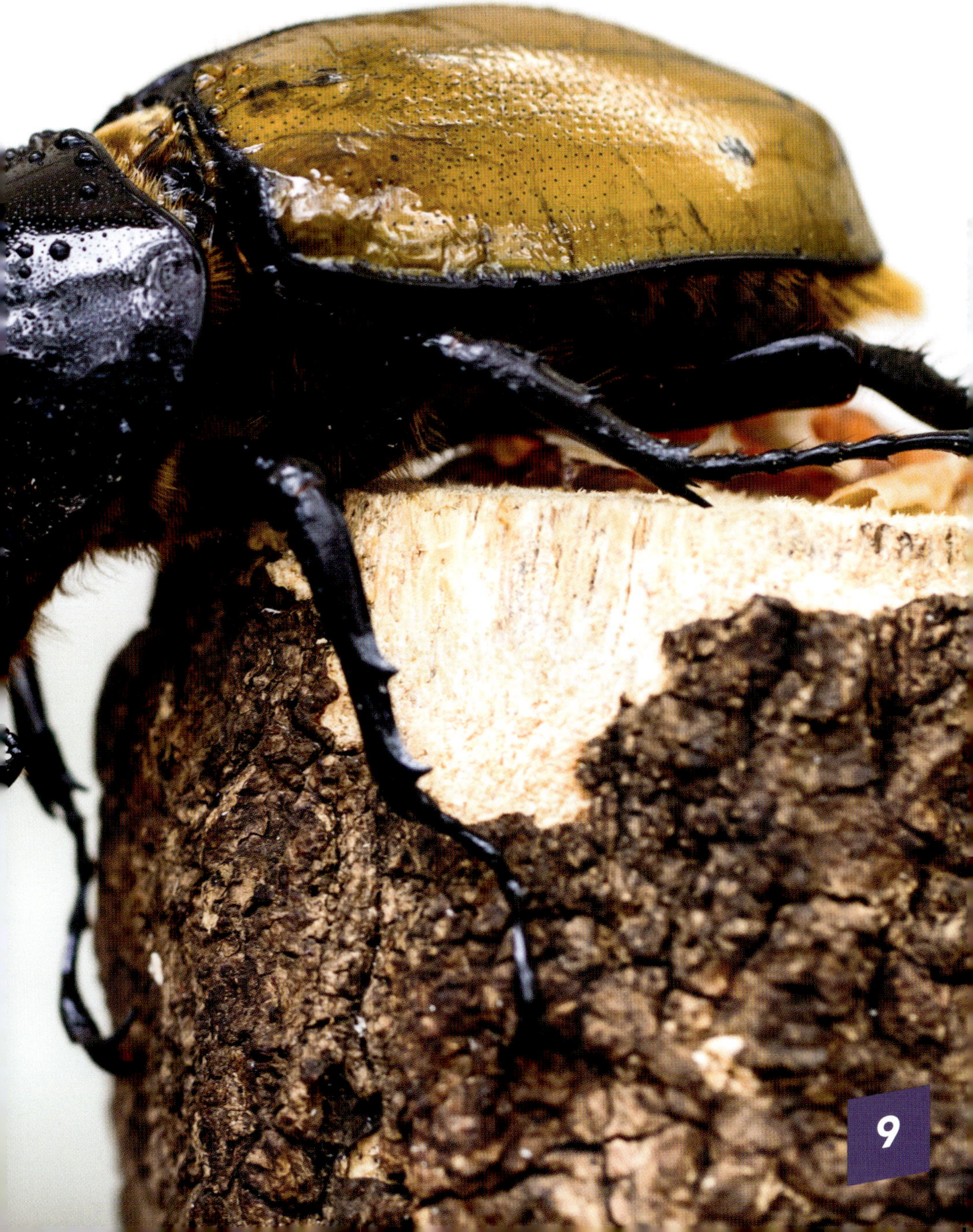

Many beetles are black or brown in color. Some have bright colors. The cardinal beetle is red.

11

abdomen

head

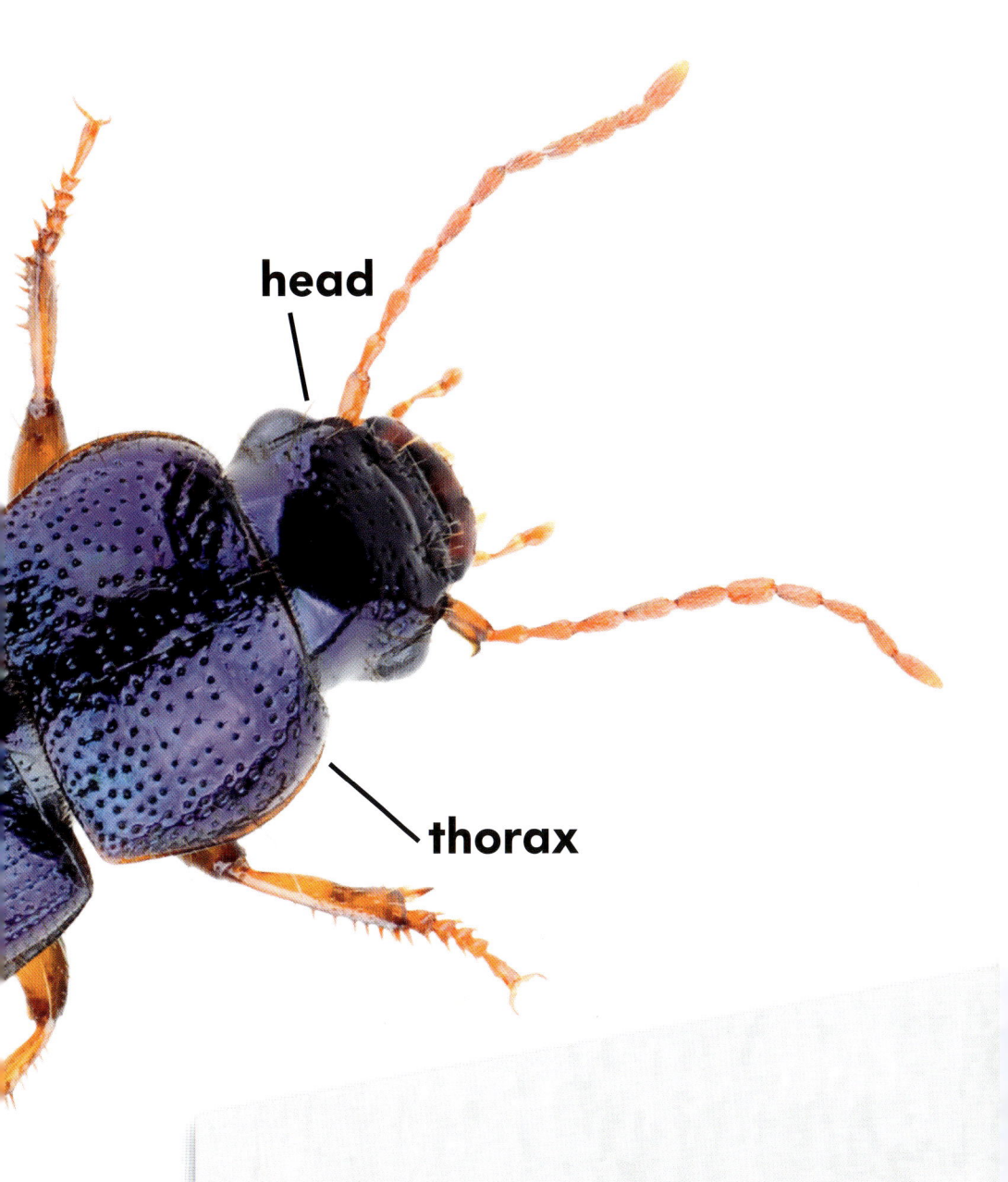

thorax

Beetles have three main body parts. They have a head, **thorax**, and an abdomen.

13

A hard shell covers the entire body. It is like armor. It protects the beetle.

15

Beetles have two sets of wings. One set is hard. The other is soft.

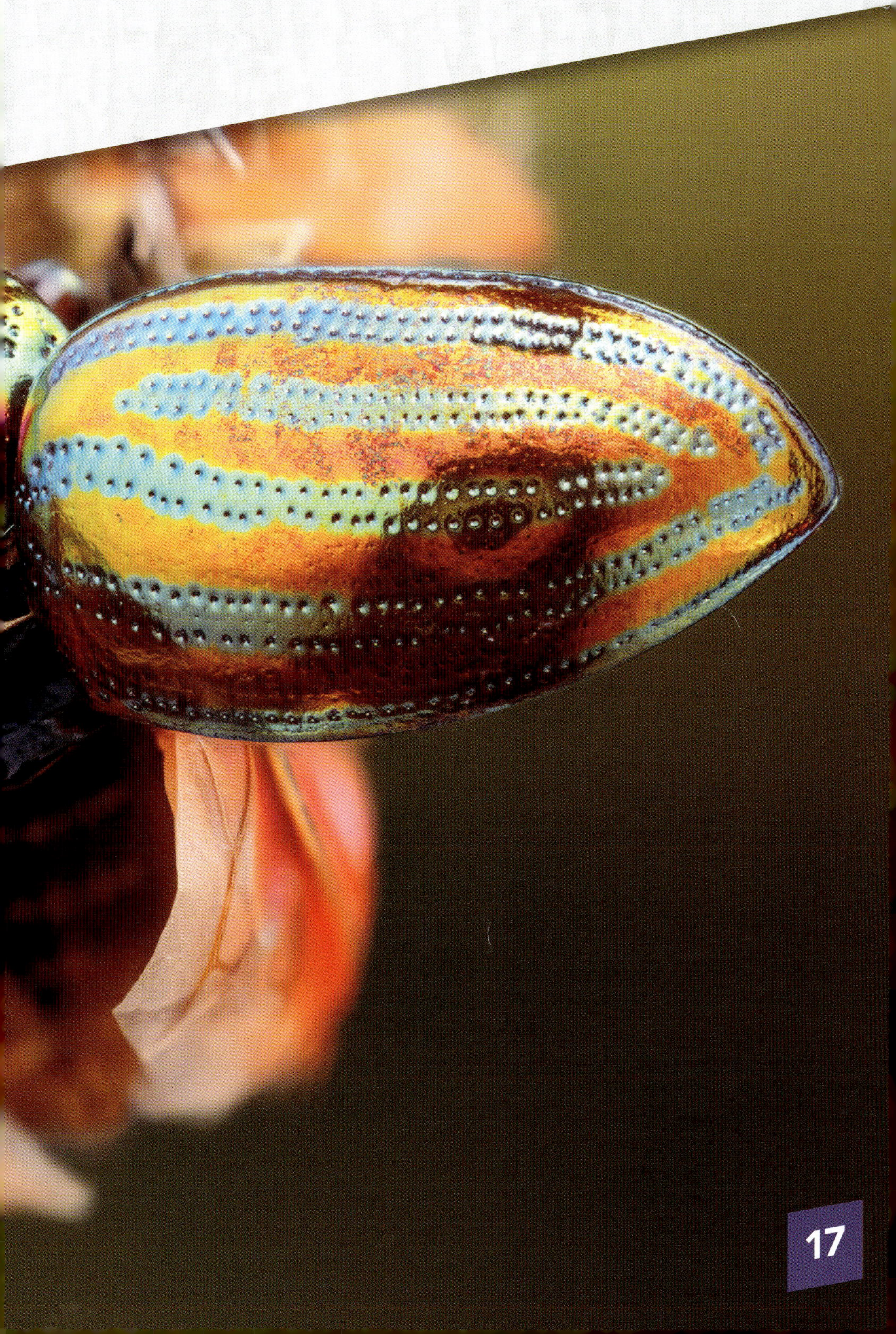

elytron

The hard wings are called **elytra**. They protect the soft wings. The soft wings are used for flying.

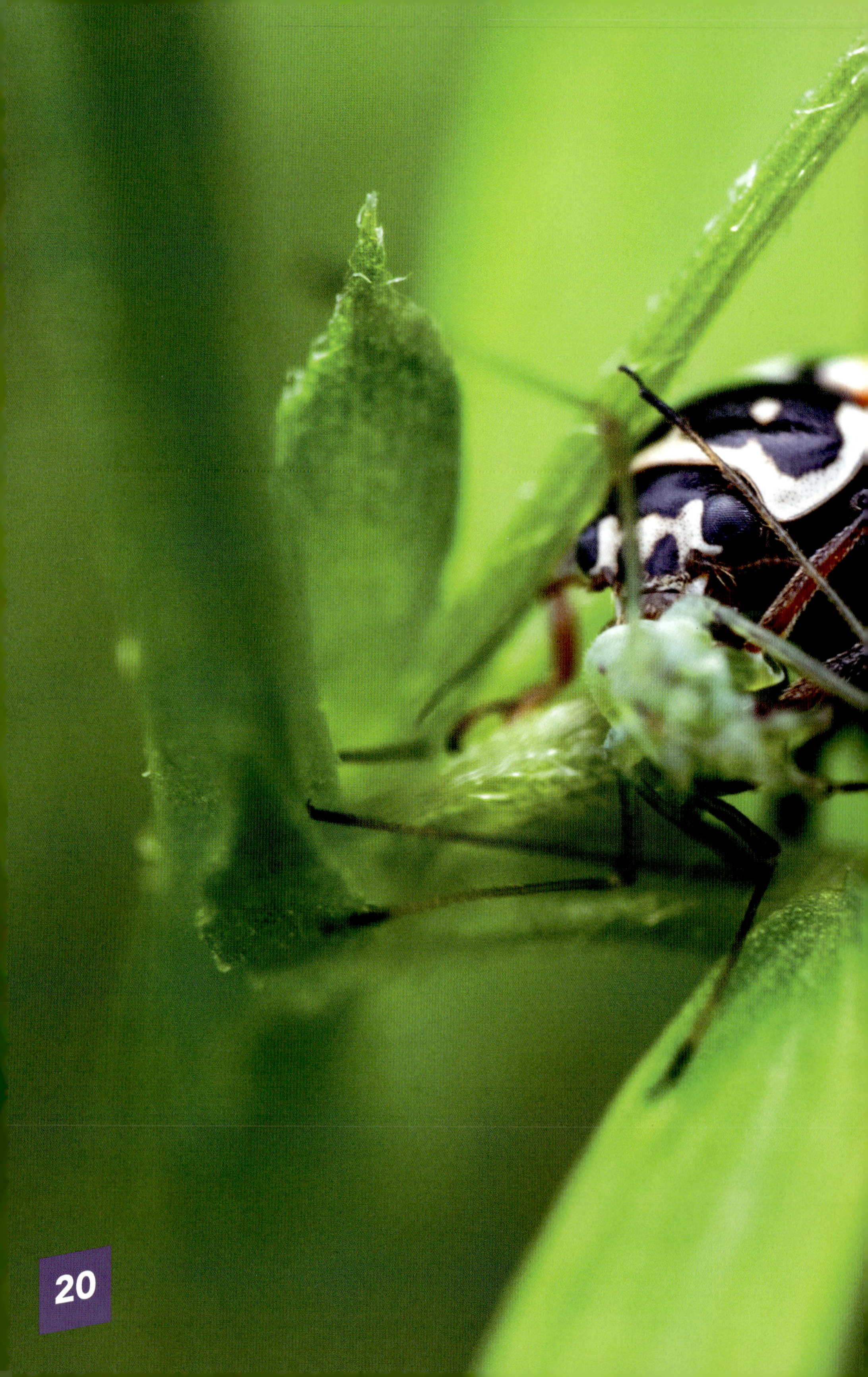

Beetles mainly eat plant parts. Some eat insects or small animals, too. A few **species** eat **dung**!

More Facts

- There are more than 350,000 **species** of beetles.

- Beetles make up more than 25% of all living animals in the world!

- Fireflies are beetles. So are ladybugs!

Glossary

dung – the poop of animals.

elytra – the pair of hardened forewings of certain insects, like beetles, forming a protective covering for the flight wings.

species – a group of living things that look alike and can have young together.

thorax – the middle part of an insect's body.

Index

body 13, 14

cardinal beetle 10

color 10

habitat 5, 6

Hercules beetle 8

flying 19

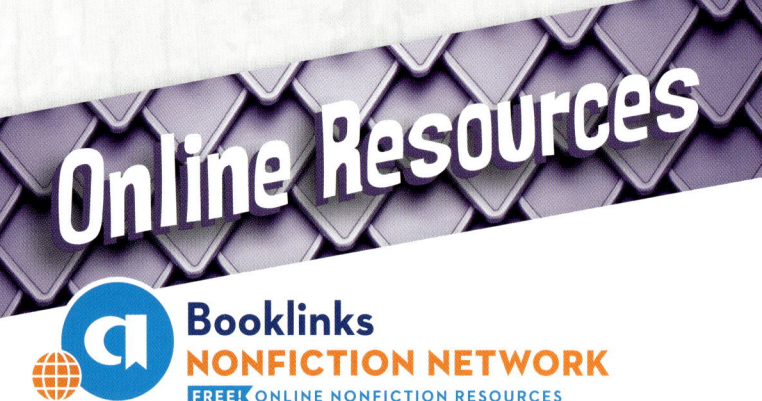

food 21

shell 14

size 8

wings 16, 19

Online Resources

Booklinks
NONFICTION NETWORK
FREE! ONLINE NONFICTION RESOURCES

To learn more about beetles, please visit **abdobooklinks.com** or scan this QR code. These links are routinely monitored and updated to provide the most current information available.